Return of the Isis

Kamila Knapik

Published by Kamila Knapik   9/21/13

ISBN: 10:0615879578

ISBN: 13: 978-0615879574

I dedicate this book to my beloved son Amadeus.

The light in your eyes

I don't want to see only twice

I want to see over and over again

So let it stay and remain.

Contents

Chapter 1
Pink and Green Ocean of Forgiveness

I saw this bright, white light, pop out in the air, right in front of me. It's like a light reaction to what I was just thinking about. I always see bright lights when there is something very important and positive happening. Like a confirmation for what I was thinking to guide me in the right direction. Every single time, up in the right corner of my eye, I can see that bright light. Like a dot or a spot, very tiny and bright.

Everything is happening at once. The absolute energy around us made it all happen. The gold light and white light. Everybody at once stood up without fear of anything. Pink and green energy everywhere, like clouds. This absolute energy, pink and green at ones turned to appear everywhere. Everyone at the unique government school 'Golden Gate' which is for only half alien and half human children, were so euphoric. We knew exactly what was going on. The whole planet Earth lightens up in colors of pink and green. Aurora lights were everywhere. Aura of the planet Earth opened to be visible to all. A number of gold and white lights also. Every person started to see each other's auras. People were jumping up and down in their pink bubbles of auras from happiness. What human eyes saw before only by a few, now all of us could finally experience. Everything happened at once. Thank God because we wouldn't want to run like crazy people full of fear around with thousands of questions in our heads. Understanding for additional brain capacity was realized right away. What has been the object of studies in countries, cultures and religions for ages has happened instantly and thank God once more because finally, we all could understand the same thing together. Understanding was no longer needed to be explained. It was common. Merciful pink and green fields of energy started to heal everybody's hearts. Massive healing of hearts started to occur without human intervention because of our intentional forgiveness in every inhale and exhale. Inhale love, exhale fear became the natural part of breathing. Forgive and forget, let it go. Like a drink of water, were water is life and washes away the fear.

We could see people on TV from all around the world feeling so happy with surprise from instant bliss. Like a rain of pink unconditional love came upon the whole planet. Collective conciseness descended upon us with all the blessings from within. It's finally started. We have been waiting for this so long. I guess we were ready for a new us. People started to automatically create their protective energy field, the pink bubble. It encased them and they began to levitate.

Veronica, the alien shape-shifter teacher, said out loud to everybody who was gathering in TV room watching people all over the world opening the pink bubble for themselves. Floating while doing this.

"The future is finally here and now." She got a big applause for this statement. "As you all know, pink and green are the colors of heart chakra energy center in the human body; therefore, those colors appeared first for all to see because hearts of all humans just started to wild opening. Therefore mother Earth also opened. The forgiveness has arrived, the healing of hearts begun. If anything goes out of control we have about 6 million shape -shifters, good aliens here in the USA and a little bit in Europe to help us lead the way to realization. Not only politicians and celebrities are the shape -shifters but the most common human helpers are in the police force, firefighters, soldiers and doctors they help people the best they can every day."

Funny because I was just thinking about the same thing how they are going to help us with this transition and I didn't realize that Alien Queen Mother was not there with us anymore. She must have stayed upstairs. I really wanted to talk to her more about everything, especially now after all this wonderful news I have even more questions. Then I heard Veronica's voice telepathically again.

"Don't worry. That was just a short visit to see you again at this pressure moment of human history. She will be back to see you soon, she said to let you know this."

I smiled back at her. I didn't have to say anything since all was understood. I think, so I am. I am what I think, I am what I eat. The message it is, in the now and here. All came down to understanding at once thanks to Creator God Himself, Herself with the most within in human body. Human body came to perfection as result of salt, light and air crystals within and the supreme alien DNA. High Mountains of crystals salt and amethyst, pink and white quarts stones. Yes, they make us younger and heather. Like a good salt lamp from the caves, yet make us younger.

Better now I choose consciously to be what I want to and not let others name me or give me the meaning which they themselves do not understand. The greatest thing now is for me, because I could actually hear really clear my baby Hazy telepathically. Thoughts sent to me by him, for me to hear only, like radio waves. I just heard him giving the whole speech to his mother over the phone about how much he loves me moreover I am the one for him. This is awesome, I love it!

Protective field of pink and green energy became like clouds all around the planet. Like a new atmosphere above. An atmosphere of forgiveness where true healing begin. Everyone was so happy and absorbed with what was going on in TV, since we all went thru this first level; it was so great to see this big change in all people's lives. Except me I could not stop thinking about Alien Queen, I just wanted to see her again since our meeting was so brief. I am pretty sure; it has to go down her way. I can still feel her and smell her. When we were still upstairs she touched my hand. I felt like some transparent echo sound went thru me. She never told me her name, but in my head I heard repeatedly, the name Isis The Mother of all Gods from Egypt along with her star Sirius. I wonder why this name comes to my mind when I think of her. Maybe this is herself? Her love and forgiveness must be the most precise in the whole universe since she knew the exact moment of people's opening of protective bubble - energy field in Pink Ocean of forgiveness. That's superb.

Veronica was continuing her speech.

"The entire world will transform almost immediately; this is only the initial step as you all know. We will require your assistance even further now to instruct and guide others. Myself, I didn't know so as this would happen so rapidly although now, we need to get ready for additional people to come here."

While the contribution of love was floating all around the air and TV, Hazy grabbed my hand and whispered in my ear.

"I have a very weird feeling in the bottom of my spine. It's like ticklish and pinch painful at the same time. Is this my Kundalini raising my love? I feel burning hot down there also."

"I think so, my love. I had the same feeling when my sleeping snake of Kundalini woke up to rise."

"Yes, but darling how long is this going to be bothering me? It's been like this for days now."

"It might take a while, I really don't know. It's all individual for the reason that everybody is slightly different."

"In addition, I started to see mine and your aura; I can see now how our heart charkas are connected. I am so in the mood to play with you right now, let's go to the cottage darling I want to practice some tantric Kundalini rise with you and lets have more of those 20 minute cosmic orgasms."

Amadeus, my son, stayed watching TV news with all his new friends and we went to have some sexy time while celebrate new beginning of the planet Earth. Funny because making love became so much easier now than before, all I have to do now is to contract my pelvic muscle and cosmic orgasmic feeling was all over me again. For Hazy was even easier since we were levitating during sexy time I wasn't heavy at all and we could do all the crazy position like in Karma Sutra picture book right there. We were almost up to the ceiling, making love and levitating when out of nowhere Queen Alien in her alien body appeared and was standing and staring at us. We both fell down on the bed since we didn't figure out how to control pink bubble energy while in distress yet.

Hazy screamed—'What are you doing here and how did you get here? We are both naked.' We cover up really quick with blanket.

"Children—she said—I came here because I wanted to tell you something very important. Actually, it is mostly directed to you Kamila because you need to gain knowledge of more respect for mothers. I cannot leave you guys before you both finally get it, as you cannot progress up your energy without this understanding."

I said—"I am sorry. I don't understand what you mean."

"I know -she said—but now you are carrying new grandchildren inside you and you both have to make sure you send to them only love because the babies are getting this energy from both of you and you don't want to send negative program to the babies. Right? Anyway you are supposed to know by now that your energy materializes much faster than ordinary people. Your energy goes where your thoughts are going. Therefore make clear in your mind what are you thinking about and taking about is positive, good for the reason that's what you making more powerful every single time. My beloved family look at this."

She went on to change her body right in front of us, it was maybe two, three seconds in real time but the complete process was so outstanding and smooth that we could see new face of Mother Queen Alien. No wonder she was still here with us because she was just upstairs like 15 minutes ago talking to us. Now she looks almost like her skin was pale white. Her eyes were smaller. Blue, green, purple, black and much taller. Like ten feet tall.

"Well, my beloved family, let me begin again. What I really wanted to tell you is that Kamila, you are right about my name, I am the Isis mother of all gods. I am in also your first mother in law in this life, because Amadeus is my grandson, my history maker, my golden grandson, my blood from my son Peter/ Charlie. Although you have a new husband now. I will show you guys later, what the meaning of this child you carry inside you is since you are not quite ready for this information. So for now, both of you give as much love as possible to your baby and as much respect to each other. At the same time as a mother you should know, there is no purest love than a mother's love for its own child. When a mother feels like she has to protect her offspring, she will kill or even die to save the child. Do you understand my priestess Kamilah?"

"Isis, my goddess—I said— so I was your highest priestess and daughter in-law too? For real? How come I don't remember any of this? I know about mother's unconditional love. I feel the same way about my son Amadeus as well as the babies I carry inside me. I just I love Hazy so much and I cannot imagine a better husband for me therefore I don't want to lose him ever again because I will not go thru this old drama again please. No separation ever again. You need to make some changes please."

"One day you will remember more and more, there is always a way up to evolve everything. Both of you are so special that you don't even know it yet, or shall I say you don't remember but really soon it is going to come upon you and you will have to take a lead, furthermore there will be no turning back because there are universal laws that are stronger than your belief system so it doesn't matter if you believe them or not. They take existence upon you, for example like gravity. You Hazy, don't worry too much. Just follow your heart with intuition. Don't hold yourself back. Push forward because you are the only one who can truly guide Kamilah to her destiny. Because both of you...oh. For real I don't want to even say this to you since you need to realized this by yourself as soon as better, who you really are. For the reason that all women aliens are waiting for you two finally open the access for us to come down. Alien males have been here for ages but alien women are here on and off only. This time is the authentic time to establish our destinies together. Sirius, our planet is dying and we have to make the final move to Earth, however, the prophecy has to fulfill first."

"What prophecy Isis are you talking about?" We asked her.

As unexpectedly as she appeared, she vanished the same way. 'Oh well', we both said and were back on track to make love again, but this time was something even more different than levitating. While we both could see our energy field auras our hearts chakras connected with floating energy one to another as before but this time all the chakras were connected. Mine to his and his to mine. We were sitting in the lotus position while making love while the channels immediately opened the energy floated in seven different colors, pink and green for heart chakra, root chakra in red, sexual chakra in orange, solar plexus in yellow, gold, throat chakra in navy blue, third eye in velvet and crown charka in purple and white. Our pink bubble of auras, connected together and we became a 12 foot energy space ball. Not like a usual aura about 6 feet per person. Funny but we automatically felt that nobody could cross this energy ball without our permission, which was like protective shield for both of us.

Chapter 2
Red snake—
the Kundalini Rise

There is something in me that won't let me sleep peacefully at night. This constant feeling like I am waiting for something. I am so tired for waiting, I don't even know for what I am waiting for? Anyway, the sexy time went out of control. Hazy started to scream again. I did not pay attention to this scream at first because I thought that was from pleasure not from pain, but when his body started to be so steaming hot, it literally burned my skin. I had to stop and get off him. I could not believe my own eyes. I had a little burn, red marks on my legs from him. We were speechless, but this was not the end. Hazy was still in deep pain and looked like he was boiling water from inside. His temperature I could tell was higher and higher, his skin was sweating, reddish along with burning smell was all over him. I could start to see a little smoke. I knew right away this was Kundalini. The red snake took over him. He could not control his power at all. The spontaneous combustion was just about to start. I didn't know what to do but to get him to the water. Consequently, I took him running to the bathroom and put him under running water. I was able to get him to the shower safely and clam down his temperature with very cold water.

"My love how do you feel?" - I asked him.

"You saved my life. Other than this, what was happening to me? I remember you told me about

Kundalini inappropriate razing can be very dangerous plus people can spontaneously combust themselves however I never thought that would come about to me."

"Sweetheart, I am learning the same way as you are right with you, all I did additionally is the tons of books I read about the entire spirituality that is happening to us right now. I actually don't know how to fix it .Maybe we should talk to Veronica?"

"You don't need to ask Veronica for help—we both heard a strong male voice. It was Peter, my ex alien shape shifter boyfriend, father of my son Amadeus, son of Isis—I am here to help you and your prime mate Hazy to fulfill the prophecy, for what each and every one are waiting for. All things have to take place previous to Isis' return as well as the female aliens, for good to the Earth. We need you like you need us. Moreover, you both, Kamila and Hazy, are very special. You don't even realize how special you are. Other than he cannot control his fears yet, this is why he could not control the rising of the red snake of Kundalini to the full potential. Although this is ok; he just needs a little help. Since you, Kamila, are his prime female. You two need each other. Anyway, you always were choosing him over me no matter what I did. This is the first time you gave me a chance, therefore we have Amadeus together. Accordingly, let it be like the wise ones on Sirius say with addition to let you choose what you want. I will do a little work on you now Hazy, so relax and let it go please."

Everything happened so rapid as always. We didn't even say a word. Peter was already pointing both his fingers to Hazy's crown chakra, along with his root chakra at the same time. We could see the silver energy coming from his fingers to Hazy's body. At first we both thought that it was just an energy coming from Peter's fingers but it looks so different and almost like some kind of metal.

"What are you doing to me man?—Hazy asked--- It doesn't hurt like before except this silver thing doesn't look like just energy?"

"I said let it go and relax, you trust Kamila right, so she is right here to help you. You know that, I am here to be of assistance for you too because like I said, your Kundalini once rose to fire. It is too hard to control, therefore we are the more advanced species. We came with the perfect solution to help you to advanced your natural potential of Kundalini. You know that without Kundalini awaking, you are living the lives of average? Of only 10% of your full potential of your brain? Kundalini awakening occurs thru deep meditation, enlightenment, bliss and also through making love. Just like you both did, but somehow even she is more ready for her complete 100% potential to rise. You, Hazy, started first to rise your red snake from the root chakra but you almost died because you were not ready like we thought. Thank god she knew what to do with you. Kundalini energy is nothing but the natural energy of the Self, the god particle, where Self is the universal consciousness as one with everything. Also you Hazy because of your fears just burned your channel of chakras. Therefore I am here to assist you and fix you up. Do you want me to help you or not? Because when you find your true Self you will become limitless"

"Yes, I do need your help please. I don't want be in fear anymore"

"My love, what are you afraid for darling—I asked him-I never thought you have fear in you. I know you panic sometimes about a few matters; nevertheless, we all do that sometimes. Please tell me what is going on."

"Kamila, zip it now—Peter said- I need to concentrate on him now please because you are guys are right. This is not just energy. This is platinum and I am injecting small sort of antenna thru his spine so the energy from root chakra where Kundalini sleeps could flow up to crown chakra and to your brain smoothly so the whole potential of Self natural power could rise in Hazy, like in you Kamila soon will also, or otherwise he will burn himself to death soon or later because of his uncontrolled fears. Remember Kundalini is slipping promise in the bottom of your spine, the god particle, given to people that one day you could be the Gods as well; this is the supremacy in you right in the bottom of your spine. Was always with you people and will never leave you because you are Gods like us. You just don't know that yet. Therefore, Kundalini has an authority of destroying you because it can also give you your true control of life. Life of bliss, feelings of infinite love and universal connectivity, transcendent awareness and creation."

While he was giving us this explanation, his body started to shape shift to his natural alien body which looked mostly like Veronica's but he wasn't so white like Isis either. He was greyer and of course his peacock feather like eyes were gorgeous. I believe this was the most eventful thirty minutes of our lives. Hazy's aura was becoming so beautiful with colors. So vivid. Plus stronger with more bright light in his pink bubble. The platinum took the shape of some kind of antenna in his spine. I could actually see thru his body inside now what was happening to him.

"Ok. I am done—Peter said -you're welcome Hazy. Although, now you have advanced your knowledge, I have to admit. I have watched you guys many times before while I was invisible to you. And I have to say. You guys are created for each other. How do you feel Hazy? Better now? "

"Oh yes, much better. Like brand new human with little antenna. Ha-ha, but what are you talking about? We knew you can make yourself invisible, but why would you want to watch us Peter? "

"Because during orgasm, the human body is so relaxed along with innocents. It is easier to see in your auras how close your progress is to your true self, especially right after orgasm which is like a golden shower of energy. I needed to know if both of you are finally ready for the next step of prophecy. Therefore I didn't have a choice."

Peter got so ecstatic talking about this. He started to vibrate and become like transparent gold, sparkling like. Amazing view for human eye to see.

"Peter—I asked—Thank you so much for helping my husband, but would you leave us alone now please? You know, we were just making some golden showers of energy for our auras. "

He started to laugh so hard. He grabbed my hand and Hazy's hand and said with a big smile on his face.

"My first ones, the show of the day is just about to begin right now. Mother of Gods Isis is coming back to this little room any second now. Again furthermore we will help you witness, what you need to see to complete the prophecy, so bear with me."

He was so right, not even a second; Isis was standing right next to him. At this moment I felt so weird because Peter and Isis were wearing little to nothing over their alien bodies. Than everything went out of control as always. Hazy and I started to hold each other so close. Not from fear but just for support during what was about to come over us. Peter and Isis raised their hands up holding together; they grabbed our hands so we form a little circle. After this energy around us was in progress, building up a field in the whole room. It was like a movie but the picture was played in 3-D. As a result, we could watch everything around us. We saw African landscapes, with trees and different animals appearing next to us. This picture started spinning faster and faster when unexpectedly it just stopped. We saw a couple of black people. Male and female, next to a big tree. They were almost naked too. What a surprise. They didn't act like they saw us. I was wondering what this had to do with us? Isis looked at me and started to speak to me telepathically.

"Do you remember anything Kamilah, my priestess?"

My mind spoke back to her. At this moment everything was on track to be put together like a puzzle.

"I remember only one flash, like we were separated while Hazy was taken from me. It was dark; I remember also his terrified eyes and my scream for him. However, I did not see who took him."

The energy of the whole picture was still around us.

"Yes, we took him form you back then but just for a while. To see if your bond between each other will grow without body presence. Anyway, this is you guys, our first creation of humans on this planet. Consequently you called them Adam and Eve, or shall I say Eve and Adam. I the Isis created the Hazy. Peter created you Kamilah. With mating DNA from our species. We did choose to create opposite sex because we wanted to see if you will be naturally drawn back to your creator. Furthermore Hazy was drawn back to me. He was responsibly following each and every one my guidelines but not you Kamilah. You by no means wanted to be with Pete. You always wanted to have more knowledge and awareness of what was going on with you rather than comfort feelings of a secure relationship with Peter. You always wanted to be back with Hazy , your prime mate, along with me the Isis as my priestess. Therefore, you became the fruit of knowledge; the apple, because you would rather bite yourself for more knowledge than me. You knew by some means that I was the Mother of all Gods, I hold the secret of creation in my symbol of flying snake. Somehow you felt this knowledge from the beginning. Moreover, you were always following me not him. Other than you were always loyal to your first prime mate as a male, Hazy. The prophecy was if you will accept Peter as your mate in addition to have a child with him knowing really who he really was, you could come back to your prime mate and create this time the perfect Eden. In addition, have perfect children with him. As well this would be the time when people will be ready to accept us- the supreme alien life forms here on Earth back with you, living in harmony and peace. Peter was improving you with more alien DNA each life time, more and more, except you by no means wanted to be with him. In addition to this, we did try so many times to move back here on earth however it didn't work because people's fears were larger than love to us. Our planet is dying, like I said, therefore we have to make a move almost immediately. After all these ages of trying this life time, finally love took over the fear to your own creator because you are finally ready to take over your true Self and limitless, potential like ours. We did create you people by mating with you and kept you separated from other intelligent species in the universe for your protection. In addition, to evolve the supreme alien race form other alien's species which are not as much highly evolved as we are. To simply protect and preserve the life. Therefore, they are not allowed here on Earth because we are protecting you as our most excellent creation until you are ready to fully protect yourself. You will not meet the other less evolved spices. Here on Earth the perfect planet, the Eden. Therefore now the most evolve intelligent life in the universe is here, now on this planet preserve, protect you and us. You are us; you are our future as well as the present. Your people presently need additional time to reach their full potential. That is all. "

After this, Isis vanishes for a second time leaving the vibrating hologram around us and only Peter stayed.

Chapter 3
Eva and Adam

We had countless questions for Isis however, Peter started to continue his monolog.

"I will explain to you everything now since I can hear plenty of questions from you. In the beginning we decided, when on Earth there was no life yet, but were great conditions for living. Like water, the most meaningful gift of life in the universe. We decided to take most of our animals and make their home here too, as well as from other planets. On top of that we created new animal species from other alien species just to explore the beautiful pallet of life. You people always wonder why all the animal kingdom of life is here, so rich and full but nowhere else, as far you know. For the reason that we as the supreme so you call alien type created this way to protect all the life in the universe and locate on this planet. Therefore, was called Eden in the beginning. Don't forget though how special you people are because you are us and we shaped you in love of ourselves. At first we were mating with you all the time but it didn't work too well. Was too much of our supreme DNA and too fast. The offspring's were becoming mutants and not developing the right way so we had to destroy them as they were too violent. At last we found the best way for you to evolve naturally along with the best light direction except it took ages. True aliens shape shifters again are mating with you all the time. We just need to skip the one generation after half alien half human is born, to have the best DNA in you. For example I, the pure supreme alien, mate with Kamila who has already about 80% alien DNA what is little bit above the average of 70% and 30% so called human with regard to the entire human population right now. We have a child Amadeus, who is now more than 90% supreme alien in him but he cannot mate with other human females who have more than 70% alien DNA because it will be too much of the alien DNA. He has to pick in the future more human than alien mate to have healthy offspring. Although, his kids can mate again with 100% true aliens. Like I said we need to skip one generation in mating with supreme aliens always in order for humans to develop in light and complete potential direction. Otherwise will not work. We know this for certain. "

"Peter" —I ask—"How come is none of your alien friends ever talked about this to Earthlings before? Why are you the first one to give us this knowledge?"

He looks at me and smiles again.

"You are my creation, how come you don't realize this yet? I am the son of Isis. I am the one who holds the supremacy therefore all of the others are just simply not allowed to share any of this knowledge. Otherwise, they will be punished and banded from here. Believe me, everybody loves to be here for various reasons. What I love the most here is beer and boobies."

"Ha-ha. Me too. Although I prefer crown royal liquor and big buts. "—Hazy said out loud.

What a conversation between two machos. What else can you expect? Following all he said it looks like we are almost the same just not absolutely evolved yet to use our superior powers. I started to wonder what was going on with Amadeus? Even though only one hour has passed. Right this second, Peter said he will go check on him while he was with his teachers and classmates. Hazy and I finally were alone.

"My love, I am so happy we could be friends with your ex"—Hazy said—"I would never expect that in million year's ha-ha. Both you guys saved my life."

"Sweetheart, you know I will do anything for you. You are mine and I am yours forever. Now we know why we feel this way. After Isis showed us who we really are, it makes me love you even more."

He smiled and hugged me so close. That was exactly what I needed at this moment, with tender voice he whispers to my ear.

"I was protecting, loving you clearly from the beginning of time. I will do this forever more because you complete me and protect me also. I speculate if this platinum antenna is going to affect me more than just for helping Kundalini rise. Do you think they can have power over me thru this metal in me?"

"Well, I was wondering about the same thing. I remember Peter told me many times he has metal in him also, so I hope one day they will teach us how to use it for our advantage, like he did for you. He saved your life baby. This is the most important."

"Kamila, I feel my Kundalini is rising once more. My pelvic muscle is starting to contract again very strong. Look at this, can you see? Hop on me now please."

He was excited all over again. I could see his pink bubble pulsate in sparkling colors. I could see thru his body. I saw his root chakra lighting up so red. At this instant I just jumped on him and we levitated as we made passionate love again. My red root chakra lighting up as well, additionally, our pink bubbles joined together in perfect ecstasy. We could mutually see one by one of our chakras lighting up to its own natural color. Root chakra in red, sexual chakra in orange, solar plexus in yellow, gold, pink and green for heart chakra, throat chakra in navy blue, third eye in velvet and crown charka in purple and white. Right after the red-white energy rose in both of us at the same time so fast from the root chakra up to the crown. Kundalini became activated in both of us at the same time. Red and white energy was flashing over the edges of our energy aura ball. Within our auras the energy ball was so colorful. Like a sparkling rainbow during rain.

Instantaneously we saw again the beautiful savanna of African landscape around us. The identical one when Isis was here, but this time we did it all by ourselves by a quantity of means… deep intense love for each other in the right place, right time. It moved us to our past. The other couple wasn't there anymore, but we saw a little boy with a little girl. We instantly knew it was our children. They were so cute, light mocha skin color and blue, green eyes.

"Hazy, I have to tell you something."

"What darling?"

"My deepest fear is what if we could not have children together? Would you not stay with me?"

"My love, don't worry. Can't you see? These are our children, besides, you are already pregnant. Why are you thinking this way?"

"I cannot do what is in front of me without you, without your love. For what is the meaning of life if one is not loved? What is the meaning of helping others if not loved? I remember everything now, what he foretold me. I didn't pay too much attention to his crazy prophecies back then when everything was normal but look at us now my love. Where we stand is just a beginning of a new kingdom on Earth."

"Remember, I love you infinitely. I even wrote a song to you about this. Please don't doubt me now."

"I love this song, I don't doubt in you. I am just telling you my feelings."

We heard a loud knocking at the door. I could already feel that it was my son Amadeus. We already have been dressed, so we could open the door with no time.

"Mommy, I was wondering what was going on with you?"

"Actually I am glad you came here alone because I wanted to ask you a very essential question. What we just learned here from your father as well as Isis who apparently is your grandmother, as you ought to already have known. Isn't that true Amadeus my son?"

He was standing exactly in front on us; I was looking into his eyes while I was talking to him. Out of the blue we lost the vision of him. Not even five seconds later, he reappeared in the other corner of the room. At this moment, we knew that all what they have said to us was the certainty. Not like I doubted them at all. It is just human nature I guess, that we need to see to believe evidence.

"Mommy, yes it is truth. I am the grandson of Isis, the Mother of all Gods. Moreover, I am very happy to be your son as well. Don't worry too much though, OK? Everything is going to happen according to divine will, as a result, all will be excellent mama."

We weren't surprised to hear about the divine will. However, this little five year old boy in no way stops surprising me. I remember when he was still a seven month old baby; he didn't crawl at all. I was worried that something was not right, therefore I went to doctor. He said that sometimes babies skip the crawling and start walking right away. So did he when he was eight months and three days he started walking, next month's after normally just running.

An extremely loud noise came from downstairs. We all resolute to come down to the TV room. Everybody was screaming and jumping again except this time it was even wilder. Veronica was talking to us but we could not hear her at all. We saw the inclusive thing on the big screen TV live from CNN reporting new changes to people all over the world. Similar to what a moment ago happened to me and Hazy. Entire attention from heart chakra energy center dropped down to root energy center chakra, like an energy ball lighting up. People were screaming from pleasure and pain at the same time, however centered and conscience on what was happening to them. Kundalini power was waking up along with getting ready to rise in all human kind at the same time. We could see policemen, firefighters and other shape shifters right on live TV trying to help people the same way like Peter was helping Hazy. Silver platinum energy was flying thru their fingers to people's energy bodies center at the bottom of the spine as well as the top of the head. Like antennas inside the spine to help the energy properly flow to the top. Most people were able to handle Kundalini rise by themselves. Even gold and platinum jewelry worn by people was able to help to control Kundalini rise because it was automatically programmed by energy field wave surrounding the planet Earth. Thru high-quality metal only, energy was able to program and save those who needed help in consciousness rise. We could see on TV this energy flow in auras stopping at the solar plexus chakra right below the chest where survivor instincts are. I don't know why it didn't go up to the top crown chakras like in me and Hazy. Maybe because people as a human kind needed just a little more time to rise up to the top. Shape shifters still were looking like humans. We could recognize them only by healing platinum energy. People were not panicking for the reason of this phenomenon. We knew somehow the new global consciousness was coming upon us. Happiness and harmony was the foremost feeling.

Chapter 4
Golden Light

Peter went back to Europe again to United Nations were he normally worked as a politician. There was also no indication of Isis. Amadeus started to play tricks on me. All the time, disappearing and appearing all over the school. Like he was invisible to me and using teleportation whenever he decided to. Transforming his energy into matter and matter back into energy in a split second. Like everything was now an illusion to me. I guess I still have a limited mind. How do they do that? This question won't leave my mind. Although I could hear Peter's telepathic messages for me though. Funny. We could hold a long conversation just telepathically. He was explaining to me what would happen next so we will be prepared and ready for it. I really do appreciate his care for me and Amadeus now, even though I do have a husband who protects me.

Because before, all things started five years ago while we were still together with Peter. I didn't understand why he was telling me this crazy stuff. Now I can absolutely relate to every little thing he foretold to me. Most of the time, he was still admitting his love for me. He was immediately explaining that Hazy and I should be together for the reason that we are made of this planet as first the strongest couple who will lead people to the realization of harmony living with alien supreme species together here on

Earth. Since Hazy and I are humans, people will trust us. If I would be with Peter, people would not trust me because they would think he was controlling me.

Veronica was no longer wearing a human body at school. She was all herself the entire time. I love her peacock color eyes. So deep into navy blue, green and purple black. Marvelous look with the gray blue skin of hers. She asked me for a walk in the park to talk to her, in view of the fact that everybody was in the TV room watching this amazing news from all over the world. The park was so beautiful now, at any time. Pink and green auroras energy floating as our new atmosphere. Like the northern lights but everywhere. With the sun light it gave the impression of sparkles all over in the air. With the moon light and the stars it became even more spectacular since pink became purple in a number of places. Spectacular symphony of colors.

"We need you to step up and take the new way for your people Kamilah. Human kind needs a new leader who knows us really well. We want this to be a woman because of Isis' return in the near future. We want them to be ready for her like you are. Since you were her highest priestess before, her former daughter in law, in this lifetime and the first strongest woman as Eva, you are the perfect fit for us. Of course, we trust you. We have prepared you for this a long time ago, all we need to do is to show to your people that they can trust you and they can trust us at the same time. Given that you already know there are good and bad aliens like humans, all over the universe. We as you are, the supreme beings on top of the life chain in this universe. You know right now people are just running around in euphoric energy as of the first week of waking up of the full potential. The process is far from over yet. People need to slow down and absorb their energy. After this, finally we can send the second wave of energy transformation, and then the third and final wave. So far only three energy centers have started working fully in all humans bodies. Heart, root and solar plexus chakras. We need somebody to talk to them and explain this process before the Kundalini rise. We have picked you. This is a great honor."

I wasn't surprised by this proposal at all. About year ago, I got this physically powerful sensation concerning this was approaching me soon or later. I didn't want to believe it at first as I knew this would feed my ego up to the selling. Thus but of course, I ignored those feelings. At this point it comes back to me once more. My destiny is calling me.

"Yes, Veronica. I know, I have to do this for the supreme life to continue to exist in addition to be protected here on this beautiful planet Earth."

"You need to discover your gold light along with an advanced knowledge of how to use it. People will really on you in addition to your knowledge about us. You don't know that much yet, although a sufficient amount that we have told and showed you already. We will continue to improve your knowledge about us. The best way for you to connect to your gold light is to start meditating again. I remember you have been practicing meditation for ten years. As well, you are certified meditation teacher. You need to go to your chamber, be still, enter your space inside you-meditate- and know that you are. It's going to work as it did previously."

"Yes, you are totally right. The last six years of my life were so crazy. Filled with so much pollution of my mind, that I don't know how I made it here with all this healing I did to my family members."

Veronica's body was shining excessively with a light of the moon along with the stars. She stopped talking, pleased herself in front of me, while she opened her hands up. This already magical night was about to tune up to extraordinary night. Veronica's hands started to let out the golden energy and created a pretty big size gold bubble. Sparkling and see thru. She smiled at me and rotated her head up, giving me a sign that it was my turn now. I felt like I can do this, since I was sending healing energy before to people. I focused on her golden bubble

while imagining light coming out of my hands.
It did work. By some means, I was ready to
create my own golden energy bubble.

"Great job Kamila. Now we can send it to the
universe since there is no one in need next to us.
Golden bubble will find their purpose and the
way to get to the most needed destination."

She raced her golden bubble up in the air
and it flowed away. I did the same thing with
my golden bubble. I wanted to create more of
that super energy healing just because it was a
great feeling to do so. Especially knowing it's
higher purpose. Veronica was tonight of the
mode to talk thru me all the possible
information so I had to listen to her.

"Pink bubble is the first level of human energy
creation, as far as protecting yourself. What
everybody is creating right now, however,
golden bubble is one of the highest healing
energy. At least for the next 1000 years to come
for the reason so as to after that, you will evolve
to a large extent and become completely like
us."

"Veronica what are you talking about? What
a 1000 years?" I was confused. I didn't
understand what she meant by saying this.

"I know, I am sorry I am speeding too fast.
But there is no time and I have to tell you so
much. I mean for the next 1000 years people will
evolve to the level of what we are now. We will

help you all the way to improve your bodies and technology. However, the whole process takes time. We will give you great tools to work with like teleportation and so on. All you need to do for us, is to learn to trust us and let us live here among you. Because we don't want to hide anymore and besides, if we will not show you our true selves, you will as a species not evolve higher. Do you understand me now?"

I was amazed by her trust in me. Of course, I did understand what she was saying. I didn't understand why me though? Why did they choose me? I can feel deep inside me there is one more reason for their trust in me. I can feel this with my whole body and my whole mind. I don't know what it is yet, but I know I will know soon. And that is how I know stuff sometimes. I can feel them inside my body, like all the time. But it has to involve me. I cannot know how to feel like this for other people. Except beloved family and best friends. Like I just know.

"Yes, I do understand now. However, I can feel you are not telling me everything. What more I should know now?"

She smiled, grabbed my hands and turned me around like a little spin dance while levitating slightly above the ground. While doing this I could see in miraculous dark but colorful night some golden sparks falling down from our movement.

"You feel well dear Kamila, but as everything needs time to grow I can tell you as much as you can absorb now with energy wise. Don't worry. It is me who has to have more patients to wait for you to learn in your own time. We will wait patiently; all you need to do is to be aware of the process of learning. That will speed up of absorbing new energy to your body."

Out of nowhere she started to create more golden bubbles faster and faster. Big ones, small ones all over the place. I didn't realize yet what was going on, however, I wanted to do the same thing, so I started and it worked. Like my wish was my command to the golden energy. The golden bubbles were floating away to destination to me unknown. It was a great feeling. Sort of a kings power trip. She still wasn't saying anything while we were performing this show. I wanted to ask her so bad. What is going on and why are we doing this, but she was so absorbed that I didn't dare interrupt her but just follow her. Finally, she looked at me as always with a cherished smile and said.

"You want to help the Queen of Aliens, Isis? You better start doing this every day. This way, we build an energy field around this planet for telepathic communication because golden energy is pure and healing for everybody. For every existing life anywhere in Universe. In our planet Sirius is still working but the planet itself is just old and dying. The golden energy will help to transform whatever is going to live there. Therefore, we have to create new golden energy field here around the Earth. It takes time. Hundreds of years to come or so. Because only the pure intentions can send this kind of energy out there. You are truly a creators hands by giving yourself to us like this with whole trust as the first one. There will be more people becoming like you because they will see the promise that lies in you. We need more people like you to build bigger, better, brighter future for this planet."

"Veronica, but why me? You are saying all this is what I already feel inside me .Like in my heart and stomach I can feel that all what you said is truth. However, I can still feel you are not telling me something that is most important about me. Why? What is it? This feeling won't leave my mind and my heart. Please tell me."

Her smile started to become bothersome to me because I didn't know if it was to tease me or to please me.

"Kamila, I have no authorization to tell you more than this. You have to wait for Isis to tell you the rest. OK? You are right, there is more to the meaning of your existence."

Veronica started to just walk away from me, while singing a song in a language that I did not understand. Happy as ever can be, she disappeared in the colorful, full moon dark night. I was still in a little bit of love shock so I stayed and watched the sky and the mystery of the night.

Chapter 5
Look at Auroras

*G*olden Gate school became more crowded for the reason that more and more people from different states came to stay with us. Life as it was, didn't change too much. Except but of course, that the pink bubble as defensive and protective energies was developing in human bodies. And we slept only four hours now. People were still driving cars and walking to work like before. Levitation became common at homes and different clubs. Shape- shifters were still not showing themselves, just patiently helping others like always. I had this strong feeling, an intuition, that Isis was in a shape shift body of Oprah as she is the most powerful woman in our time. Helping others as a true angel, sharing the knowledge and compassion for everybody. Hence far, only a couple of them showed me their true bodies and human bodies they shape shifted as living here among us. Veronica among other teachers were teaching others step by step how to control their pink bubble and more energy exercises. Like she has explained before, absorbing true self energy takes time in order to work in the best direction. People intuitionally knew, felt somehow, about shape shifters existence after how they did help us in the true first step of Kundalini rise. We began to trust them, for the right time to give us an idea about the rest of the process. From this point, every night all the people in the school who knew how to create this the most gorgeous energy,

were gathering outside and sending golden
unconditional love to Earth to create protective
and communication field. Consequently, our
telepathic abilities grew a little bit more,
however, not in the long distance for humans
since the protective shield was just building up
by us. My pregnancy was going very well. I could
actually see my babies inside me. Yes, Hazy was
very happy for us to have twins. Baby girl Aurora
and baby boy Luc. I have eaten so much water
melon during my pregnancy that I felt like I
became one. During the birth I was only with
women around me. They were all standing
around, and sending me golden energy so I
would not feel too much of the pain. Aurora and
Luc were so precious healthy little angels to us.
Hazy was so proud to have a son, and I was so
happy to have a girl. Amadeus was the most
happy for the siblings to play with. The twins
were about one year old, when the things started
happening again. People were ready for the next
level to rise up. Everybody felt this way. People
were talking about the next level all the time
now. All over the world. It was all in the air, or
better to say in the new atmosphere all over the
Earth. Now visible to the human eye, colors of the
rainbow mixed with golden and white sparkles.
The aura of the Earth. During the day and
night the field was getting bigger and stronger.
Sunsets and sunrises became poetic symphony of
colors. Like the most beautiful paintings. We
were gathering during sunsets and sunrises to

absorb the strongest, healing energy from the sun. To help us evolve quicker within our true self to rise. The whole planet became one big rainbow again because the rainbow was given by the creator to everybody, not only to select ones.

Amadeus was so happy to see his siblings growing up. They were already walking and talking a little bit by now. Luc's favorite word was daddy and Auroras Deus short for Amadeus. They were glowing in pinkish and golden right from the start. The pink bubble was activated right from their birth.

Kids all over the world had the most fun now more than ever. Somehow they were the ones who developed their new abilities the easiest way. Maybe because children minds are less polluted with bad programs and stereotypes like adults are.

Veronica asked me and Hazy to go for a walk next to a lake. It was during the day now. There was a nice place to sit right next to the water. The view was amazing but Veronicas weird smile was bothering me because I haven't seen this smile before on her face. I have to ask her what is going on. She just smiled bizarre once more and said to me.

"Let's all go into the water I want to show you guys something exceptionally important yet again."

She laughs so hard that's it really continuing to bother me. Hazy said

"Thank God there is no sharks here because I wouldn't get into the water. "

While we all were standing quite deep into the water Veronica pulled Hazy's left ear. I was just wondering what is going on. Suddenly he froze. I was so stunned I didn't know what to say.

"What did you do to him Veronica?"

"Nothing really, this is what he really is. A robot."

"What are you talking about? All this time I was in love with a robot? How is this possible? Please explain to me because right now I am really confused. I cannot believe this. Why?"

Veronica started laughing again and it really became bothersome. My heart was so much in pain now even more than before. I didn't want this to be reality. She started to explain what was going on.

"Well my dear, you need to understand one thing. We as the supreme alien race were mating with your people for thousands of years now. What brings us right here to this very powerful moment of human history however, is not the first time when we are trying to reach your consciousness as well as show you who we really are. Most of the times in the past you just thought that we are gods or some mystical beings after our teaching to you. You still were choosing the darkness instead of light we showed you. What's more, we have made so many promises for you simply because we love you and care for you. One of the promises we made for you was that you will live forever like us while reaching the highest conciseness. However, there is a war behind the seeing world between the light and darkness. And if the soul chose the darkness and Mr. Evil D. We cannot help but to remove the darkness from the soul so the remaining light can still live in the half robot half flesh body here like Hazy. Possibly one day if ever we need new souls, we can still give a second chance as a soul. But till then he has to remain an inactive light in robot body. Simply because he will just do more mistakes. You can still enjoy him as dancing robot, sex robot, cooking robot and great protector. Since his soul had so many great lights in him and because of our promise to you that you will live forever therefore we cannot just send him to darkness."

I was speechless. This is not what I imagined for a husband at all.

"If that is the case, whom I am pregnant with then?"

"This is another story that I will explain later, OK? Please process this information and when you think you are ready for more I will let you know. More to the point I heard you saying many times that he was giving you the best sex of your life right? Well now you know why. Or you know I will tell you. How you are pregnant with yourself ha ha. Do you get it?"

"Veronica, are you crazy? Does he know he is a robot?"

"Not really. Because than everybody will know what is going on. Furthermore, this is not the right time for this to come to the pass. Soon, very soon though. That's why I invited you here to talk about it."

We were still in the lake while Hazy wasn't moving and I really wanted to feel his hugs. Now more than ever I felt sorry for him. I couldn't stop but wondering what he did to deserve this robot life. All I knew in my heart and my soul is that I still wanted to help him. To give him a chance to be the whole soul again. If what Veronica was explaining to me was the truth. This whole alien supreme life is so confusing. I rather thought it would be simpler than that. The water in the lake became darker. Wind started to blow stronger. A number of big clouds were passing by the sun. Veronica's eyes became more serious, she was about to start her monologue again. She pointed with one spinning finger to the water and a water spiral came to life very close to us. Not a big one, but still powerful. At this point I knew that most of what is happening here on earth was controlled by them. The question was which of them were good and which of them were bad aliens? How do I know to distinguish one from another? I guess I have to recognize them by what they do not promise. I don't know of a better way to find out who is who.

Veronica pointed with her other spinning finger to the other side and made additional water spiral. Consequently now we have two water spirals on either side of us. I have to admit that it was an amazing view. Also amazing feeling to watch her performing those things. While she was still controlling just with two fingers the water spirals she started to talk to me.

"You see Kamila; you can do the same thing as me, only if you really want to. It's all in you already there. Consequently, it is in everybody, the question you just asked yourself a minute ago. The one we have been asking you now for ages. When are you going to decide to choose the divine light in you instead of darkness? "

Because only light will take you higher and higher. You see, we were trying so many times fighting for your souls with the bad aliens here on earth. What you understand as today's myths, or even some of your real history. Still, after all the knowledge we gave you, you try to convert it into darkness. Therefore, this time war will be invisible to you for the most part. We will get rid of the bad alien shape shifters. For the reason that reality is required to become reality as it knows, so we can all live happy together here. We have to make it this way because we have tried all other possibilities and it did not work. All while we were showing you the fight over your souls and you still were choosing the darkness. "

"Veronica, are you saying that there is a war here on earth now and we don't even know about it?"

"Yes, this is true. But this is all you need to know for right now. You will see only the final fight so you can know who won and whom to follow. This you must see in order to get more light into this planet. "

The water in the lake calmed down now. Like the whole speech of her resembled the water spirals. The sun came out and the rainbow showed up in the lake next to us. The other end of the rainbow, which was fuzzier, was touching Hazy's body. He looks like a rainbow robot now.

"Kamila, one more thing today I have to tell you. You are invited to Chicago's biggest talk show. You will be talking about your first book, as a cover up of course; however, you need to send them a message about what I just told you. You can do it in a more nicer and plausible way if you want. They need to know at least this much."

"What about Hazy and the kids?"

"Don't worry about him. He is programmed to follow your directions. The kids can stay here with us or go with you. Your choice."

"You mean I will be on Oprah?"

"She is a very good friend of mine for years now. Don't worry everything will go just fine."

"You mean Oprah is one of you?"

"Oh Kamila, I didn't say that. Therefore ,don't put words to my mouth OK? I think it's time to wake up Hazy. He missed out on so much fun with us. Ha-ha."

"Ok, let's do this, but I don't know how. You have to show me."

"Oh Kamila, this is piece of cake. Just pull his left ear and say his name. "

Consequently I did what she said and Hazy woke up, like nothing ever happened, with a big smile like always plus ready to go. We had to go back to our cottage since we were all wet now. I didn't know if I should tell Hazy what happened or not, so I decided to wait for a better moment to tell him what happened. On the other hand I wanted to see how he would react if I told him he is a just a robot. After a long bath we took together, I couldn't wait any longer. My curiosity was just taking over.

"Hazy, what if I told you, that you are actually a robot and not a human being?"

He started to laugh so hard, he didn't stop for a while. As a result I laughed with him but it was kind of sad to me at the same time. I share tears from my eyes too. Obviously, Veronica was telling the truth about this one. I couldn't stop but wonder how many robots are here on earth right now since there are about 6 million shape-shifters. She never told me how many of those 6 million are good or bad aliens. Consequently many questions came into view. My mind was going a thousand miles an hour now. I did like it on one way, however. I wanted to be at the end of the path and know the answers to my uncertainties. I guess I have to look for the bright side always. Look for the light. Look at the auroras around us that already came out of this planet to protect us.

Chapter 6
The Lion

We decided to take all the kids to the big show in Chicago. After giving it some thought, they all deserved a little bit of the spot light. The flight went well, with no major problems with the little ones. Amadeus was very helpful and playful with Luc and Aurora in the plane so as a result of that, the flight went really fast. I have never seen so happy seeing Amadeus while playing with his siblings. I was so nervous to speak in front of such a big audience and being on TV like this to the whole world basically. However, after a while, preparing my speech in the back I felt more confidant. Finally they called our names and it all started. Right before we were about to step out to the stage, Oprah appeared next to me and whispered to my ear.

"Don't you dare tell them who I am, she smiled and walks away."

The show went quite fast. My speech went exactly how I wanted. I was talking about my book 'Love, Sex and Aliens'. People were laughing at my little jokes because I introduced Hazy as my dancing and sexy time robot. Along with Amadeus, Luc and Aurora as supreme alien's children. Most people learned how to control their pink bubbles by then so the whole audience became like a playground after a while. I was demonstrating how to create a golden bubble in addition to what is the use for it, like Veronica showed me at Golden Gate. To the delight of several people in the audience, they were able to create their own golden bubble right there. Now everywhere were golden and pink bubbles. I felt like something really big is going to happen right there in front of everybody. Hazy stood out in the middle of the stage and from all of his fingers, silver, white energy started to come out to create a pretty big size ball. It looks like silver, white and golden spots were all over. People were happy to see this ball, for some reason I was too. The ball started spinning really fast, creating more and more light. All of a sudden, from all people in the room, one by one solar plexus chakra opened and connected with the beam to the silver, white ball. Hazy's body and mine did the same thing. He started dancing plus singing a Bob Marley song. I am the rainbow too. To the rescue here I am. This was so funny because everybody started singing and dancing too. Like disco dancing in the 70's. While we were all having so much fun, TV's national news were showing the same thing happening all over the world. Where silver, white balls were created by other robots I guess, as well as people were opening their solar plexus chakras the same way we did to connect with the beam to the ball. In every silver ball there was a different song to dance and sing to. The whole planet became for a minute, a disco dancing karaoke. Still, we couldn't tell who was who since the shape shifters didn't make themselves known yet. I didn't know if people believed me when I told them before but after this for sure it would be more plausible.

We all were exploring the new abilities of our bodies, energy wise for the next ten years. It was fun for the most part to everybody. Hazy started to teach people how to control metals and create different useful stuff from it. People learned a lot in this short period of time.

Amadeus become a young teenager now. He was so tall like 6.5 or so. He loves to play basketball all the time. The time he spent with Luc and Aurora as well as the other kids in Golden Gate, was just playing and fooling around making silly jokes and pranks on everybody. His favorite was to appear out from nowhere scaring me to loud scream. Being invisible I guess, was one of the highest privileges for supreme aliens. I wonder if we can eventually achieve this ability too. Amadeus wanted my hugs and kisses all the time. Like he needed more than average attention. I mean loving energy. His love and understanding grew to the point that we all felt his longing for something we could no longer grasp. The entire Golden Gate community became a first fan of Amadeus for the reasons of fun and playful time he tried to provide for us for the last ten years. Most of his spare time he spends with children developing new kinds of games and sports.

We were all waiting for this day for a long time now. The Final day of summer little

Olympics at the Golden Gate for the kids. All kinds of athletic children were attending for the last few weeks hoping to win the competition. Of course Amadeus' favorite was basketball since he was very tall. Which gave him a huge advantage. It was beautiful day. Sunny with no clouds in the sky. Only the planet's new aurora atmosphere of rainbow colors was the perfect daily decoration now. Like a perfect day was falling to the end and the final game was performed of basketball. On the field during the game, an unexpected huge lion appeared while Amadeus along and his friends were playing on the field. Everybody started screaming at first.

"Lion, lion, run away!..."

For some reason, not understood to me at this moment, Amadeus was the only one not screaming and standing still right next to the Lion. I was quite far away from him, so basically I could not do anything.

"Amadeus, Amadeus, run away! What are you doing?"

His friends were trying to scream to him. I thought that he just froze from fear or from shock. The Lion did not move. She just was standing proudly right there. Amadeus was moving towards him even closer.

"What you doing Amadeus? Stop!" People were screaming.

I felt peace in my heart. While watching this crazy wildlife situation. I connected mentally to Amadeus' heart and he was so happy like I've never seen him before. Amadeus spoke his words now.

"Dear friends, do not be frightened by this beautiful Lion. This is my grandma, the Isis. She just wanted to make a big entrance like always. Therefore don't worry, everything is under control. I haven't seen her like forever in her real body so she just wanted to make it very special for all of us."

The public were not laughing for some reason. I guess none of the shape-shifter supreme aliens took an animal form in front of them before. I didn't think of it this way before either. I guess it's like they did in Egypt or Greece prior to this. I suppose so. Amadeus was still speaking.

"She wants to make a particular announcement to you all. Furthermore, I am here just to introduce her. My beloved ones. Here comes my dearly loved grandmother Isis."

The Lion sat up on her hind legs and raised her front paws up. Like a standing position for humans. She was huge about 8 feet tall or so. The lion's body began to change colors to white skin and reduce in size a little bit to human corpse like kind. And there she was beautiful grand Isis. With her white pale skin and peacock colors eyes. This time she had on a white shall with golden ends on her as her clothing. She looks proud as well as joyful. In her expression we could see a smile on her lips. She spoke;

"Welcome, everybody. I am so happy to see you all. "

People started to cheer up and applaud her while she was talking.

"I will make this short and straightforward. What I came here for is to make things comprehensible for you all, so you won't be wondering what is next with this whole planet take over. Let reality become reality right now. Therefore, my only grandson, Amadeus, will take over in the near future to lead you to the highest level of consciousness. I will make him a president of this planet when he is ready. Accordingly, you better listen and help him right now. Because he will be the one who will bring all people, robots and supreme aliens' together living in perfect synchronization and happiness."

People did not bolt from the blue at all. Neither did I. We all felt that he was quite extraordinary from his unusual behavior and his blood line. I wasn't expecting this so soon though. For me he was still just a little boy. I guess from the mother's side he will always be this way to me.

Isis continued her speech;

"Do not push him though. He knows exactly when and what to do. I am here today for the reason so you will not contradict him when he will call for you the most. Get this message to your heart and never forget. For when this time will come to pass, you all see what I see."

Silence was deep after this one. Like whole space and between froze in time for a minute. Even Amadeus wasn't smiling at all. His face was quite serious and thoughtful. He stepped out take hold of Isis' hand and shape-shift in front of everybody. Even I, as his mother, didn't see him like this before. He almost looks like her. But he was much taller now compared to her. Same skin and eyes like her just taller. I don't know if that was because of his age, but he just extended from his human body to his supreme alien body. His friends started to laugh out loud, so it broke this restless stillness. Kindly cheering the whole performance the children started to come out of their seats and move to the field where Amadeus and Isis were standing.

"Amadeus, Amadeus rock me Amadeus...."

Their favorite song was again on their lips to hear, while they were walking towards the center of field. What a spectacular day. I never was more proud of my son like today. Tears were falling spontaneously from me in high spirit eyes. The game wasn't officially over but I guess it was over now. It Did not matter which team was first. For today both teams were first in summer Olympics in basketball.

While all the children approached Isis and Amadeus, Veronica came to me and whispered to my ear.

"Watch this one now dear priestess."

Isis and Amadeus started to create golden bubbles faster and faster. Spontaneously all the children around in the circle did the same thing. The whole space was filed with golden bubbles. Like they learned to do this in just one second. Isis spoke again.

"Build this golden energy field every day now, like I did . This is your new reality as well as the future. It will create a new protective atmosphere around the Earth. In view of the fact that today is after a short ten years since the solar plexus has opened everybody bodies. You should do this to simply support the planet we live on. You should understand that this is the commandment of all existence. Otherwise, you are wasting your time to the darkness where you do not want to be left alone. Because the gold light is here and now to the rescue so you better make the best choice for your existence and follow the light. Walk on golden light. Walk on gold so it will become reality. I say again to you all outright. Let reality become reality. And love my adorable grandson Amadeus.'

At that instant, all the children came out of the audience to the field and they all started to sing their favorite song. Amadeus, Amadeus rock me Amadeus. On and on, louder and louder. Clapping hands and walking around in circles while Amadeus and Isis were in the middle of the field. Even the basketball coach was dancing in the middle along with all children.

While the kids where dancing and singing, Isis and Amadeus started to levitate together while spinning. The golden bubbles were all over now, making an unbelievable most spectacular show. Since that was an open field, the bubbles started to float away slowly up to the atmosphere to build up the protective filed around the planet. Everybody was so happy and cheerful. Isis, in her natural body along with Amadeus floated towards me and Hazy. She started to talk to us mentally.

"I need to see you both in the conference room on the seven floor, now please. Bring Veronica with you. We need to discuss some important information."

"Yes Queen Mother." We both responded

I guess we both could hear her at the same time. Wow what an awesome feeling. So robots can do that too. Well, its sounds reasonable and understanding to me after all the explanation about the robots. Amadeus stayed on the field *along with all the partying that was going on right now Hazy and I went to get Veronica.*

Chapter 7
See Thru the Truth

We could not find Veronica in this crowd; however we could see Isis flying right to the top of the school building. The golden bubbles were acting as steps as she made her way over there. She was stepping on them, floating and walking at the same time. Finally I saw Veronica next to the basketball coach; she was still in the middle of the field, where the entire crowd was. Well, I thought, maybe we should just levitate there also, since everybody does now, it's not such a big deal anymore. Hazy as he heard my thoughts, grabbed my hand and slowly we levitate towards Veronica. She smiled at me.

"Kamila, aren't you the most proud mom on the planet?"

"Oh, yes sweetheart. I feel so overwhelmed with joy and happiness. Isis asked us to see her in the conference room on the seventh floor. She is already there waiting for us. "

"Ok then, let me just tell the coach to go with us. «She said—I was surprised that she wanted to take him with us, but trusting her words I was just waiting for them to join us.

"Charles, my dear fried—she said to him---it's time to see the Queen now."

The four of us floated away on golden bubbles to the top of the building. I didn't have a clue, as usual, to what was going on but as I learned, everything is happening for a reason in these times and especially here in Golden Gate. We went to the conference room where Isis was waiting for us, sitting now on her golden chair. I was wondering. Just who was the mysterious Charles basketball coach now? I didn't have to wait too long. Isis and Veronica instantly turned off Hazy to stand by control and turned on the projector light out of his solar plexus to the Charles body. I could see instantly all the bodies he shape-shifted while he approached me. It was quite a few of them. There was Peter/Charlie, Amadeus' father in the basketball coach's body. They always try to trick me at first and then tell me the truth at the right time and moment when is obviously needed. That was reasonably a second show of the day for me. Ha ha ha. Peter spoke to me.

"Kamila, did you really think I would leave my son? That would never happen. He is the most protected person on this planet along with his sibling twins. We are here to make things right this time for this planet and for the people of this planet. Therefore, nothing or anyone can stop us. So don't worry my friend, because every little thing will be alright."

Yes? Guess what? You probably know what happened next. Hazy turned up the Bob Marley song again. Baby don't worry, every little thing is going to be alright. That was very sweet of him. I mean Hazy. Everything was like a day dream to me now. I couldn't see who was who and why they did things they did. However I felt like they protected me too. Isis turned Hazy back to his normal sweetest thing ever. I started realizing now why they gave me a robot. But still didn't know who the real father of Luc and Aurora was. Isis turned her face to mine very close this time. She spoke to me.

"I will give you what you need now. All you need to do is to share this knowledge with your people. I will give you glasses thru which you can see who is who. I mean good aliens, bad aliens and robots. About immortals we will talk last. Remember there are six million aliens you will recognize good by the golden pure energy they have. The bad ones, you will know and robots very simple. See here you have the glasses you can see who is who. Put it on."

I put on those normal glasses look alike.

"OMG, Isis you are made from gold. You are all gold."

That was weird as I could see all the energy, all the way. No more secrets. Well, as far as I was concerned. Because they always come up with something more to show me. Of course in the right time. Funny because without glasses she looked normal again. I mean alien look. White pale skin and peacocks eyes. She spoke to me once more.

"Don't worry. Every little thing will be all right because Hazy has those glasses built inside him. He knows who is who. His mission is to protect you and the children. Also, don't ask me who are Luc and Aurora because you will all see at the right moment. Just be patient. It will come to you spontaneously. Take those glasses now, moreover you will visit our dear friend on the Chelsea Lately, show in Los Angeles. She is waiting for you. Take your book as an attention grabber and tell your people about the glasses. They need to buy just regular glasses and sun glasses too and wait. Because when the time is right we will turn them into the one I just gave you. With the energy wave flow. That will teach them to trust the right people and protect themselves. Do you understand Kamilah my priestess?"

"Are you for real Isis? OMG, this is awesome, like Amadeus would say. Ha ha ha."

"Yes, it's awesome—she smiled---There will be one more trip you have to make to those talk shows. To Los Angeles again to see Ellen. This trip will be the most extraordinary. You will take Hazy, all your children, Peter and Veronica. She as well as Peter will explain to you later what you will have to do. First we have to see how people will react to what you have to say to them. Okay?"

"Wow! I cannot wait for this one. I am so excited. I always wanted to see Los Angeles. I need to go and start packing. That's wonderful."

Hazy was also very excited. We went to pack right away after this. We make sweet love right after packing, I guess out of this all excitement. I didn't ask him but he tied me up for the first time. Legs and arms open to four corners of the bed. He was very gentle with me but made love to me for a long time but I couldn't levitate. During sexy time he was almost screaming at me. I felt like he did something energy wise to me but for some reason I could not see this time.

"Do you really want to know who is the father of your twins? I am. I am"—he repeated this three times. I was shocked because I knew he is supposed to be a robot, but why did he say that? I didn't know how to tell him this. All I knew is that I wanted to try again.

"My love Hazy, this might sound funny to you but Veronica and Isis showed me you are a robot. I saw how they turned you off and on for various occasions. You didn't even realize that. I am so confuse now. I wanted to believe that you are the father of our twins, but please explain to me how come this is possible."

He smiles to me and when I see his smile it makes me the happiest woman ever. But this smile wasn't gentle, he was angry. He spoke again.

"You only see what they want you to see. When will you realize this, my love? I have to do whatever the Queen says. Do you get this or not?"

"I am so confused baby. Please don't be angry. I love you so dearly and I am very happy with you. I don't want to change this ever." — these words calmed him down, he smile again. But this time the sweet smile, the one I truly love.

The trip went just fine. California is so beautiful. Filled with nature. The shore lines are the most beautiful ever. My favorite was to watch the albatross with those funny blue legs. So cute. The children were very happy to travel. They enjoy most trips away from home. Chelsea Lately, was incredibly entertaining as always on the talk show. I was a little shy at first to step out in front of the public, however since this was not the first time, it all went well. Everybody was laughing at my little jokes and when I told them about the glasses they laughed even more. I just really hope they will buy at least a pair of those glasses for one dollar so one day they will see what I can see now. As Isis promised to me. We will see. This might be one of their tricks. You never know for sure with them, since they have all the technology and knowledge. However, I believe that would be very helpful for people.

On the way home Hazy was behaving really weird. I knew he wanted to tell me something he just didn't know how to start. So, I hugged him and kissed him. I said.

"What is wrong my love? Please speak to me. You know the best way to solve the unspoken misunderstandings is just to say them. I promise I will try to understand."

He smiled at me, kissed me back and spoke to me.

"Are you ready for this? Because I wanted to tell you this for a long time. You need to know this and people need to know this as well in order to recognize the confusion. At first it might sound silly but this is how it works. Isis told me to tell you this after the show, so I guess now is the right time. You know my past when I was experimenting with the forbidden. I really don't want to live this way anymore because I have you and our kids, however I have to warn you so you can tell others when the time is right for them. Those bad forbidden aliens set up their way of communication in our regular language so normal people will not understand, but they would understand each other so they don't have to use the aliens language in front of them. "

"My love what are you talking about. I didn't see any of the bad ones yet?"

"Not yet, listen to me now, and tell your people later. Ok? Now only a few of us can communicate telepathically because of the protective communication field around the earth is not set yet for everybody. Therefore, some of them have to use regular speech like people. And it works this way. Remember that silly movie 'What Women Really Want 'or something like that? When yes means no and no means yes. When never means forever and forever means never?"

"Yes I recall something. It was a comedy about some guy when he started to hear women's thoughts right?"

"Yes, yes that's the one. I know it's confusing and funny but this is the way they had to communicate and make the false promises. So they can lie and do whatever they want. "

"Wow, what a bummer. Are you for real? I know those Hollywood movies can have a message somehow at some point from aliens but I didn't imagine that this is going on to that extent."

"My love, you need to learn faster about the energy flow. I thought you knew that already? How the energy works. Energy never dies, but only transforms. I know I said never, but this time never means never because it's all depends on your intention of what you mean in your heart. "

"Well then, let's set new code. When we say three times never, never, never. It will mean never and so on. Because after three times is a pattern, and it repeats. Well in mathematics at least, which is the true language of the universe. Or we can say where no mans no and yes means yes. Where never means never and forever means forever."

"Kamila, yes that would be very true if they have only the purest intentions but they can just simply lie and change a meaning of three no, no, no to three yes, yes, yes."

"Yes, you're right my love. Well I guess we need to trust each other and learn more about the flow of energy in auras what the colors mean when people are producing their intentions while thinking. The time will come when all is clear and intentions will be visible and understood. I trust you and I trust you and I trust you. Is that good enough?"

"I believe that our love and pure intentions will set us free. Please forgive me about the forbidden stuff I did before to you and others."

"I know my love, you were forgiven the first time I saw you. Oh yes. I understand now when Veronica said that the people will not see the war this time because they didn't not follow through with previous attempts of setting freedom. I get it now. Thank you my love."

"Ha-ha you are so funny. Now you get it finally. I am so happy. Well there is one more very important thing Isis said to me to prepare you for but this she will tell you herself."

"Ha-ha you are so funny. You think that I don't know. I remember more and more now and I won't do your job on forbidden because it doesn't work on me. You believe that those two wooden statues you hide on the sixth floor will bring you happiness. Ha-ha. Then you need to destroy them because I don't need to go thru anything to be with anybody. Love always should be given unconditionally not thru the forbidden."

"I know, I was just waiting for you to say this. It's all already done my love. I just wanted to show you so you know the truth and how my story all started."

"Thank you darling. I know your story. Peter told me about it a long time ago. I just didn't know what was going on back then. However, now it all comes down to place."

The end of the flight went really fast. After all this information and emotions in public places, as well as in the plane, I was ready for some rest. The children were tired also. We went to bed right away. Well, except for Hazy and his robot programmed endless pleasure for me. I love it. We were almost sleeping when Isis show up again. She turned Hazy on sleeping mode and started to talk to me however this time she was not even smiling.

"Listen to me and listen well, Kamilah my priestess. Because I will not repeat myself again. Hazy told you the introduction to the most important message I am here to give to your people thru you. Therefore, do not take this lightly."

Oh, I was kind of petrified the way she change her look while she was talking to me. Her eyes were black now and her skin color was changing constantly thru all the colors from white, black and rainbow colors. Only the eyes were all black now.

"Yes, Queen. I am listening to you very carefully. I will do your will." She continues.

"Kamilah, my dearest. Since you finally know that Hazy is a robot and you have absorbed the information we have given you so well, I can tell you the truth about your twins. "

"Oh great! Finally, I cannot wait to hear!"

"Well, I know you figured out this by yourself before, I think you just didn't want to be so bold to say it out loud. Well, I did put something in Hazy, since he is just a robot. My seeds were in him and Aurora, she is golden like me. Luc however has different seeds than her. They will show their energies when in the right place and time comes. However, before that, we need to help people of this planet. This is the last time we are doing this for your people as you should understand who you really are. We as the supreme immortals, the aliens as so called by you humans. We don't have to live here. We can pick one of the millions of different planets. We don't have to go thru this drama of saving you again. This is the fifth and last time we are doing this for your people to finally help you understand who you are. Because you are supposed to be ready by yourselves now. We are all from the same God particle. This is not about the alien DNA about to save your human DNA. We have different planet colonies, set up ready for us with less advanced human kind to live on. We don't want to destroy you at all, we want to give you so much more than you can imagine but first you need to want that and trust us as your own kind. You know already there are good and bad aliens the same as people. Just to show you how to control your energy is enough because if we gave you more and more advance technologies you will end up destroying yourselves. You need those glasses to know who did what for real not for just illusion."

"I heard this theory about saving planet Earth and human kind by the fifth time on the Discovery and History channels before. It was very interesting."

"Interesting, oh you say? Well, I am glad you did because this is not a joke. We are all tired for endlessly trying to save you all. How are we supposed to communicate with you people when you don't want to listen? Yes, there are many movies which are pure imagination; however tons are not. They are a message to you all. When will you finally get this in your heads? We don't have to live here. We are here again because what we promise to you. However you need to want to give us a real chance for peace this time around otherwise I don't really know what to do with you."

"What do you mean you don't know?"

"Doesn't matter now. I have a second gift for your people. What do you think? Will they buy those glasses and wait to come true what you told them?"

I was thinking to myself- why all this pressure on me, why can't she do it herself if this is so important?

"I can hear you Kamilah. Great question but I have already explained to you this one before and I don't like to repeat myself. They will not trust me if they would see me like this. The fear in people is still there to trick them from the truth. You need to tell them and show them because you are one of them. It's as simple as that. I will come back in this form to show them more, in the right time and place and you don't need to know about that yet at all. Too much information for everybody at this time and place is not good."

She was even more upset now. Her eyes become red and her skin navy blue. I wasn't scared but I didn't like it. I preferred the way she looked before. She was prettier.

"Well, you thought right Kamilah. No one likes to see me like this, even myself. Don't worry. I won't hurt anybody. I will give you something very, very special for the people of Earth soon.

Very soon. This will be teleportation devices and receptacles as well as the blockers to where they cannot teleport. How about that huh?"

She woke up Hazy now. He look at me and smiled like he knew what was going on and said to us.

"That is what I say. " He started to laugh very loud.

"What is going on with him Isis? Does he know what is going on or not? I don't get it. Please explain."

She looks at me like I was crazy now. Finally she comes back to her white first form and spoke to both of us.

"He is the best robot ever Kamilah. He is programmed for years and years to come to do what needs to be done for you and I. No worries at all. Just pleasure with him. Remember? Ok, I will come back later. Just snuggle and make some sweet love with your hubby. Next time you see me, I will give you the devices and tell you exactly what to do and when. For now take care of your children. I will see you soon."

She disappeared as always as quick as she appeared. I was just wondering how am I supposed to do this, and tell the world about it? I guess it will come to me in the right time.

Chapter 8
Crystal Castles

Amadeus and I were on the lake at sunset watching the mesmerizing colors of the sky, just sitting and enjoying the moment. He was hugging me, assuring me that everything will be just fine. The whole planet was going thru the next big step of transformation of the main energy coming down to Earth. He projected for me the view in front of us above the lake which was playing out on TV. The world was wild right this instant. We could watch it like it was on a big screen TV.

I got my glasses on therefore I saw who was who this time. The robots and good shape-shifters were gathering in the middle of big cities where the old government buildings were. They were forming circles, holding their hands. There were many of them as many as the old buildings were. Some of the small some of the bigger depended on the size of the buildings. The beam of white light went thru all of them. Great show watching this all together happening at once. I wonder what a rush people were experiencing while watching this next to the buildings.

That must have been an amazing feeling. People were cheerful after all these good things happened. They naturally trusted and could see the great outcomes of this. Beam of lights became wider and more numerous, like they were teleporting something bigger and better on those places. Colors were beginning to change to each and every one of the pallet of pastels along with the golden freckles. From these beams of light colors began to come into view some shapes of new buildings made from all kinds of valuable stones. I could easily recognize the white and pink crystals, amethyst, emerald, diamond and all different category of precious stones along with the golden monuments.

The new buildings were breath taking, totally not from this world. People were standing, hypnotized just by looking at them. Many people were wearing sunglasses and regular glasses just for this event. I guess they listened to what was told to them. I am sure they could see now who was who.

The white house in Washington DC was the last one standing alone. Old and nothing changed yet. Emotions were reaching the maximum. People knew that something different will happen to the white house. On TV, live reporters went totally out of control with comments and predictions of what would happen in there. The old world was coming to an end and the promised new world was about to come back finally.

A gigantic beam of white light went thru the whole building and instantly, as if from above, a solid gold Castle appeared. In just a split second this time. The other buildings took a good five to ten minutes to transform into the new ones.

After all the new government buildings were in place, people who happened to be there for the purpose of work, emerged from the new buildings all healthy and untouched. Along with the shape-shifters, however still in human bodies. People all around were amazed by what had just happened. TV news reporters were going at the speed of light now with comments again. But this was not the end of the changes. Not even close.

From the water at the sea shores, enormous silver globes emerged and came into view with thin tubes connected to smaller silver globes. Like some type of constrictions or new kind of buildings. With a golden shine all over. None though came out of these structures. Everybody started to wonder what they would be for? After this, just outside of the towns and suburbs, the same kind of silver with golden shiny big globes appeared from the ground and were lifted up on strong large poles. They gave the impression of being like modern windmills but much taller and bigger. Tall as the most modern tallest buildings in the world. The new architecture was absolutely exceptional. Somehow it all fit together very well. I mean the new and the old buildings.

Amadeus and I were holding hands really tight. He was in very high spirits. Joyful and cheering for the moment. I was still astonish and almost paralyzed by what has happened. We could still watch on his mind made TV projector people that were going inside of the new government buildings. The view inside was even more beautiful than outside. All crystal transparent floors. Different stone colors, all the colors. Each building was as if it were made of a majority of three or more stones with gold and diamonds as main decorations.

Nevertheless, the silver, golden towers were difficult to get into. No one came out and no one could get inside yet either. People were trying to climb in from curiosity; however, they were too slippery and unreachable. There were neither doors nor a sign of any possible access to it. The surface was spotless, inaccessible all around it and up to the top. We all were wondering why this is? On the other hand no one was too suspicious or in fear because of those circumstances. Rather hoping for something really superior, since only excellent things have happened so far.

We went back to Golden Gate. Of course, everybody was excited and out of control with pure happiness. Luc, Aurora and Hazy hugged us for a welcome. That was a very sweet and touching moment. We went back to our cottage for the night. However, lots of kids, parents and teachers stayed up the whole night watching news from the whole world. Hazy and I were doing the same thing but from our bedroom. Everybody was astonished and memorized by what happened.

New laws were set by shape-shifters. More suitable and easy for people to live with. Marijuana and alcohol become legal again for eighteen years and older. Well, me with Hazy totally agreed with it. Since before it was so absurd to let the eighteen year old teenagers die while fighting for our freedom. But they didn't have the freedom to drink before they die on the battle field.

We don't have to eat too much now. Appetite was less an issue now because of the light energy we could feed on from the crystal castles and golden light we created and fed on at the same time from the protective field. Crystal castles are the most marvelous creations people have seen. Because those other, still mysterious, silver golden globes were just very modern and simple.

Years passed buy and the globes were still unopened and unreachable. They started to change colors with silver and violet to purple from time to time. People stopped wondering what was going on with them and we treated them like some kind of new statues on the land and sea with mysterious, but good meaning.

There must have been some galactic movement changes because one day we woke up and the moon, actually two moons, were much closer to the earth. Like the whole solar system had changed or something. The view of the huge two moons and sun was totally breathtaking now. As if from the fairytales.

Chapter 9
Immortal Angels

Now, several more years have passed by and our children were having children. Being a grandmother was fulfilling and a heartwarming experience. People were in high spirits. One day Veronica, Peter and Isis called me and Hazy to the seventh floor for a significant meeting. All three of them were in their supreme alien bodies. Isis was more golden than ever, her entire body and aura was one gold. She spoke.

"Here is the booklet of how to use the teleportation devices. You will have to go to that talk show I told you before and introduce a copy on live TV."

"Oh my goodness, for real? And where are those devices?" I asked with a surprised smile.

"Well, you don't trust me?"

"Of course I do. It is just I want to know how we are going to do this?"

"Don't worry about a thing. Everything will be shown in the right time. Just take your whole family, along with grandchildren, Veronica and Peter to the talk show and upload a free copy on internet during the live show. Make sure everyone sees you do this. After it is done, we will give you the devices to teleport. You will have to show them how to use it as the first one, so you better read this on the way there."

"You mean I will have to teleport as the first one to show people how it works? And where I am supposed to teleport myself to?"

"Oh, this is the question; you need to answer to yourself. Here is the booklet. Go now. Read and make sure everybody is ready tomorrow morning for the final trip."

Veronica nor Peter, or Hazy said a word. They were smiling to me with exceptional love. Like they totally knew before that would happen today. At first I thought it was a joke or something but as I started to read this short booklet I knew they were not teasing.

Of course, everybody was ready the next morning. Veronica and Peter were in human bodies this time for the trip. We had a nice flight. I might say the last flight by physical plane so to say. Ha-ha. We were energized; particularly children and grandchildren were blissfully joyful. There were several cars waiting for us at the airport. The ride to the studio was even more amusing. The enthusiasm was reaching its zenith in all of us. When we arrived at the destination, Ellen was outside waving at us. She was told before what we were supposed to do here, what Veronica told me before.

We all went right to the main studio. The audience was waiting in their seats and the show was about to begin. Together we went right to the stage. A gigantic applause welcomed us, with great music as always on her show. First, children were talking about loving energy and introduced their children. After this, Veronica handed me the device, which appeared similar to a silver cable tied together. built for a head size with a couple of buttons on the side. Peter was holding a second identical one, smiling to me. I knew he was about to put this one on my head. When he did so, Hazy imported files of the handbook to the internet, as a result everybody could read and see us on live TV.

I wanted to make this short in essence. I didn't want to talk too much in view of the fact; they could read all the manual explanations on the internet now. I told the public I am going to teleport myself to Poland and bring my brother Michael back with me because I had the second device in my hand. We video called him and talked for a couple minutes from the studio, and he agreed to it. The historic epoch was about to come to reality. I wasn't frightened at all. I had complete confidence. People in the studio were silent and motionless. All I have to do now is to press the bottom and mentally say where I wanted to teleport myself. Consequently I did. In a split second, I was flying like in my dreams. In the tunnel of white spirals. A second later I was already in Michael's home. Everybody gave a loud wave of applause and joyful scream. They could see all on video call from Skype on a big screen TV in the studio. Michael was like.

"Sister, awesome job. You are something. Now you want me to fly with you back there, ha?"

"Well, everyone is waiting for you. Are you ready?"

"Of course I am ready. Let's demonstrate to them what it is like. Optimistically thinking, we will make use of it for righteous purposes."

"Yes, let's pray for this. For the better, brighter future for each and every one. "

"Ok, sis. Let's do it."

We held hands together, closed our eyes and imagined the place plus address. Ha- ha. I didn't remember the address but I knew where we were going, so did he. Once more, we flew through the tunnel of white spirals for a split second and we were back in the studio. At this instant, the public went ecstatic. Confetti came raining down on top on us. We were all stunned by what happened. More TV's came on so we could see the wild comments from the whole world. At the same time, live breaking news came about the silver-purple globes that were opening.

Yet again, everything was happening at once. Supreme aliens with their natural bodies on came out from the now shining with gorgeous colors globes, with tons of teleportation devices. People gathering around the globes got the devices right there. More and more aliens and devices came out from all the globes in the whole world at once. People were running now to the globes to get there as soon as possible. There were no lines because the devices were floating in the air so anybody could just grab one or two at the most.

Veronica whispered to me and Hazy.

"It's time to go home now. People will go a little wild now with their new toys so we better hurry. I have devices for all of us. Therefore, we will get home safely."

Peter and Veronica gave them to all of our family. When everybody had the devices on their head, we all said—destination Golden Gate. All of us teleported securely home. People were reading in haste the instructions on the internet. The mathematic explanations were for them to figure out though. I didn't have a clue how this thing worked. Despite the fact that we were home, we wanted to watch what was going on in the world now. All simultaneously we went to the TV room. News from the all over the world were going silly. Especially in Asia, China. Something weird energy wise was going on there. Resembling the golden clouds we were creating before. Now more cameras were concentrating on those clouds. They were approaching the shining globe towers. Golden clouds got bigger and bigger. Tons of them, however, only in China floated next to those towers. Out of the golden clouds came out humongous oval, balloon shaped crafts, masses of them. They were teleporting those crafts to Europe, USA and so on to all over the world. However, there were just floating nothing yet came out of them.

Ellen video called us thru Skype with a number of questions about the floating balloon craft. Veronica, now in her natural looking body was about to take this call, however Isis appeared. Her whole body was gold this time. She wanted to take this video call live and broadcast it from Ellen's studio. She didn't even wait for the questions. She spoke instantly.

"Yes, those are very, very special crafts. They hold millions of our supreme alien's babies. People of the Earth who will adopt those babies love, take care of them as of their own, will gain the immortal bodies as we have now, after this life. You don't know this yet, but not only the soul can be immortal. Bodies as well can be immortal if we want them to be. Those babies will grow only up to 40 years-old but look like young bodies and 10 feet tall. There will always look 30ish, 40ish young. Furthermore, they will stay this way as long they like those bodies. You people of this planet will gain this blessing too, as well as you will listen to your pure hearts intentions and not hurt each other or us. There will be more and more technology given to you. This will given to you by my grandson Amadeus who will be the new president for planet Earth now if you want. I will give him a voice now."

Amadeus came to the cameras and took a stand. Smiled with his beautiful body that still looked human. He was as very handsome now as a grown man. He spoke.

"If you want us to stay here and live among you with peace and harmony. I will guide you and direct you what and how to do it. I will give you first the deviances of the protection field from the teleportation devices so as homes, business and so on could be secure. Consequently they will be protected from thefts and unwelcome with this new technology. However, first you need to adopt our supreme babies and love them as your own or even more. We know who we can give them to. We know who has the purest hearts of you people, so don't take offense if you will want one and not get one. There will be many other chances to prove yourself for a better, brighter future and raise your Kundalini to seventh chakra, where illumination comes thru your bodies. Those who would like to adopt the alien supreme babies along with the protection from teleportation should go to the shiny globe towers now please. I will guide you from there. Thank you. And remember we love you all. All we want from you is to love us back. See you soon."

Isis turned off the live video cam. Still we could see what was going on in the studio and other TV stations. At the present, people were playing with the new toys as they teleported themselves everywhere. Now robots turned to robots, shape-shifters to alien's supreme bodies and people were still people. Some immortals, were looking like human kind some of them like 10 feet tall supreme aliens. Alien's babies were pinkish, white. Human similar bodies, but they were so much more shinier with their golden auras all around. Citizens were in progress of getting-together next to the silver globes. Further, more were teleporting themselves to the meeting places to pick up the babies.

Isis came to me and Amadeus. She spoke to us.

"Kamila, I can hear those questions in your head. Let's say those facts. Alien mothers with the babies were in China for long time hiding now. It was safe there because no one really wanted to be living there from the western world. They were working hard for years as everybody else for less pay than here. Our planet Sirius, is much closer to exploding now. Therefore, we had to move each and every family here before people could decide what they wanted. We could choose other planets to settle in for the new home. However, we like this one the best. Amadeus will guide people in the right direction for all of us."

"What do you want me to do next Isis?" I said.

"You my sweet priestess, now just give good loving energy to your children and grandchildren. Enjoy the years off watching them grow. When you and your husband Hazy pass away, it will be together same day. The next life I will give you after what you did the immortal bodies. Even to him, everything will be forgiven in view of the fact that he helped you all bring to the end. Where end is, is a new beginning. Beginning of the new world on planet Earth."

Amadeus was very glad for the reason that nations were gathering next to the silver-purple globe towers. He was prepared to give another speech. I could tell by the look on his face. Supreme aliens were just waiting for the speech from him to give away the babies along with the protection devices. Amadeus was ready so the were people as well.

"I hold on to your hearts and see thru your pure intention about a promise for a better, brighter future for all of us together. As I speak to you now, the planet Sirius, where they are from is about to explode. I am one of you and one of them. I have human blood in me. When you take all the babies into your hands one by one. It all will be done. The end of Sirius, the explosion of their planet is the beginning of the new Earth now. Energy from there will get here in time for additional technology advances we have for you. Please enjoy and respect the new endless possibilities in your life now. I will see you soon."

THE END